COPYRIGHT © 2020 PAUL PETILLO

ISBN: 978-0-9829593-6-7

For my wife, Bonnilyn

Introduction

Part One

Blink

Dot/Dot/Dot

Closeness Nearness

A Poet I am Not

Save

Page One

Devil in My Backpack

Pathos

Stamped by Seasons

Part Two

Our Entry for the Hottest Couple, 1992

On the Porch, Underneath.

About the Author

Whisper Me

A Collection of Poems, both Long and Short

Paul Petillo

INTRODUCTION

I should do as other writers do, but I am not other writers. I often look at my body of work as a painting, one in which I often want to add another brushstroke, a shadow here or there, a color that might seem a better fit. I suppose I can be forgiven, but I am not seeking forgiveness.

Each day that we age adds a different perspective. This could be why day-to-day no longer applies to our overriding personalities, mine included. It might be more hour-to-hour, even minute-to-minute.

I now have numerous works in the public domain. It is an eclectic collection of works; some adhere to a genre – such as my contributions to the world of finance and investing, while others do not. My fiction is a self-exploratory journey, as I suppose it is not all that unusual. Rarely do writers create characters that do not carry some latent trait of the person writing the tale. So that's not an oddity.

I tend to write about isolation. That has to do with my mostly disastrous childhood. My first three novels, a trilogy, dealt directly with that subject.

And isolation prompts and search for love and inclusion even as it attempts to be indifferent and reclusive.

I also tend to write about religion. I am an avowed atheist who has a fixation about God. I explore it using old documents. In 'On the Porch, Underneath,' I pull directly from Thomas Aquinas's 'Summa Theologiae' as the point/counterpoint source.

My latest work, a collection of novellas, continues that exploration with three characters who do what they do alone and are not necessarily aware they need human contact.

And then there is this work of poetry. This effort is about love – I have found it with one woman, and I have dedicated every work to her. I will do the same here as well. The poems in Part One were sent to her one year for her birthday, a different one (and style) each day. It was me playfully illustrating the world as I see it with her in it.

Part Two is also about that love, but differently formatted and approached with a more nuanced eye. "Our Entry for the Hottest Couple, 1992" was written for a local contest. We won, and we were pictured in the Oregonian on Valentine's Day that year.

"On the Porch, Underneath" is a long-form exploration of my deepest fear: losing her.

This publication is also urgent. You have isolation, God, love, and urgency, but not the way you might think of it. I hope you enjoy it.

PART ONE

BLINK

Blink

She has remained with me
        well beyond what logic might think.
And during those decades
        that slipped by,
                relished, but in a blink.
So fast, we hurtle forward,
        Too focused to look or reflect on the aft.
And in between, I wait
for the next time I can hear you laugh.

DOT/DOT/DOT

Dot/Dot/Dot

the ellipsis suggests that there's more to be said,
a dangled three dots of a thought that is read.

and read what you will into what is portrayed,
what is not spoken has as yet been conveyed.

and if we suspend out thoughts for a sonnet
we live for the life that is lost in the moment

so we stop and enjoy every second we have
for the last is the first love and the first is our...

CLOSENESS, NEARNESS

Closeness, Nearness

"See that one," I say pointing to the blackness above.
The ambient light shrouds all but the most brilliant but from here.
On a blanket, on the grass, it is a canopy of light.
"Which one?" she asks
and the closer she moves.
Her skin touches mine and I try to
memorize, a memory clear

As the sky, stars moving away, aged of a long-ago night.

"The one that is blushing," as her closeness, nearness wove.
And every detail stands out, and some blur, how to steer,

I ask myself, to love her more than a minute ago just seems
right.

A POET I AM NOT

A Poet I am Not

My memories eidetic, makes me wax poetic,
Though a poet I am not.
I could seek your absolution, and make a resolution,
A Poet I am not.
With a rough attempt at rhyme,
in crude pentametric time
A Poet I am not.
With her each day I travel, seeking to unravel
A Poet I am not.
If you chance to see her eyes,
you'd also realize,
What I find so scorching hot.
Not a moment dares slip by, without telling her just why
Her love's a passion's knot.
With the best days yet ahead,
with many words unsaid,
She knows I love a lot.
And as time will mark her birthday, I thank her for another day,
A Poet I am not.

A Poet I am Not

A Poet I am

A Poet I

A Poet

A

Save

Save
Occasionally, she leans into me,
And thanks me. And even as sincere
She tells me, for saving her.

To save I know is to free;
To liberate is one thing I hear
She tells me, for saving her.

I would defend from enemies I see
And ransom, and extricate and clear
She tells me, for saving her.

But it is what she did; unshackled me
And if I emancipated her from fear
She tells me, for saving her.

From the peopled world we both flee
I protect from a vulnerable tear
She tells me, for saving her.

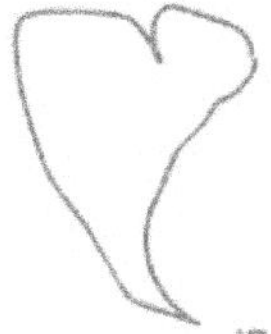

And as she leans once again into me
I tell those dangers "stand clear"
She tells me, for saving her.

PAGE ONE

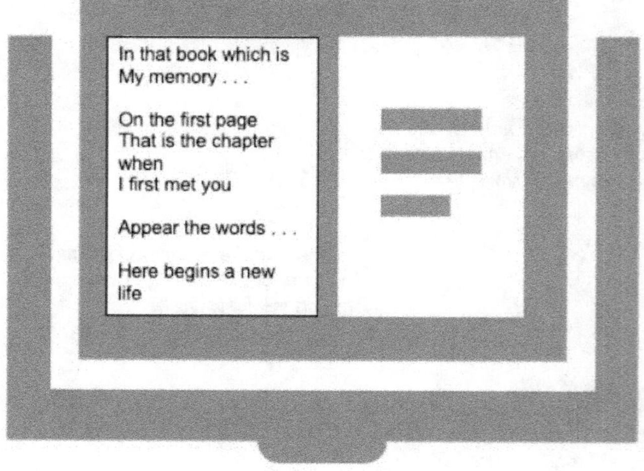

In that book which is
My memory . . .

On the first page
That is the chapter when
I first met you

Appear the words . . .

Here begins a new
life

THE DEVIL IN MY BACKPACK

The Devil in My Backpack

To suggest this is a journey, a linear path of sorts,
point a to b;

           but then you realize
that each moment is another opportunity, a chance
to kiss her skin,

    to memorize.

And although the time we've had, and time to come
headwinds aside, I'm proud to confess
there is more to each successive step –

        as long as you are my only
      address.

And what of the world that each day I enter,
the me that I bring to the place.

Is it the I are we and we are us,
    evidenced by the welcome embrace?

        The devil in my backpack, my past in tow
        I now left where she suggests; at home
        where it belongs, replaced by the man
        you see.

You'll never know the man she owns.

PATHOS

The voice is used for attention,
for thoughts outside of convention.

To suggest this is normal,
with her touch so informal;
her love is a marvelous
invention.

And yet with that all the
intrusions,
she makes sense of all the
confusions.

In my universe, she's my sun,
a galaxy of one,
time proven, this is no illusion.

Wading gently into the chaos,
yes, she adds meaning to the pathos.

Awash in emotion,
I swim in her ocean;
with her, a celebration of Eros.

Love is often portrayed as floral.
With words that are pleasantly aural.

But the truth should be known,
it's impossible to own,
unless it is love shared as plural.

STAMPED BY SEASONS

Stamped by seasons

one
    by one,
    we became one;
Whisper me my love.

PART TWO

OUR ENTRY FOR THE HOTTEST COUPLE CONTEST, 1992

I hear him get up,
and I roll to his side of the bed.

I feel his warmth, hugging his pillow.

He stumbles through the darkened house, turning on the heat, making coffee.

I hear him shower,
-and I wish I could shake off my slumber and join him,
-but I doubt he's left enough time for that.

Although,
I've made him late before!

I hear him set my alarm,
-then gently sit on the side of the bed to say good-bye.

We kiss and embrace.
He smells clean and inviting.

He tells me he loves me,
and I tell him that "I love you too."

Much later,
My coffee,
and love note await me in the bathroom.

My work demands that I get up early.
I make the coffee and put it in a hot pot
and leave it in the bathroom with a note.

The note is simple enough,
"I love you" or "Thank you."
This morning,
I write it on the mirror with soap,
-and frame it in a heart.

Before I leave, I will wake her to say goodbye.
I get a kiss, or three, and warm, sleepy hug.
I tell her I will call her,
and I will.
Just to say, "I love you."

Whenthe phone rings,
I know it's him.

My day,
is about to, blur and disappear.

He will ask me how my day is going,
and I will tell him if we need to talk later.

He will, if needed, make time to offer his uncanny insight.

We never discuss serious business on the phone.

He will tell me his day is going fine,
but he wishes he were with me.

-I wish he were too!

We tell each other we love us. It's kind of an electronic hug and kiss.

I look forward to his call at lunch.

I call her on my break.
We have a rule
-about this conversation.

Nothing heavy.
Not about money or work or kids.
From experience,
we know these topics usually take more than a few
moments – to discuss.
We schedule a time.
I will ask her how her day is going,
and she tells me she misses me. I tell her I love her.

I may work at home,
but the outside world leaks into my domain.
I hear,
-sad tales of relationships,
-separate vacations,
-separate nights out.

It is beyond my comprehension
why someone would want to do something without
the
Pleasure of the company of their mate.

Why bother
if the sharing will only be the retelling
or not
of a life and experience that did not include them.

And why
do they continuously invite me to join them in
their need

to "get away?"

I don't try to explain.
They wouldn't understand.

My life is and with my husband. It is us or nothing.

I like thinking about him.

PAUL PETILLO

I walk through this life insulated.

I must carry this aura,
That says, 'there walks a very happy man.'
It must show,
and
judging from those around me they would like to
know how to achieve it.

I wish
I could tell them the secret.
But they already know why I am like this.

I'd be envious too!

I often leave work on a mental journey to her to re-
live a moment
Or
to plan a future one.

Then I wish,
I could call her,
or better yet, be with her.
I decide to buy her some flowers
And I am happy to find I have just enough money in
my pocket.

It will make her smile.

We embrace.

I melt,
and he knows it.
I'm already crossing out some of the less important
topics
we should discuss tonight.
We cook dinner
together,
as the kids flock to tell him, seemingly at the same
time,
how their day has gone.
He listens, and talks to each one of them,
and,
when they aren't looking,
he grabs my butt.

That man needs me
And he has way of telling me
all
the
time.

The flowers   make me smile,
and without a word but
I love you.

I know there won't be much room later in the
evening for talk.

Then the kitchen
becomes a mass of young bodies with tales to tell of
their day.

This is hero worship any man would die for.
We conjure up dinner, touching each other the
whole time.
A brush here,
a touch there.

After dinner, I will read bedtime stories to our
youngest.
She showers,
and I wish she would have waited.
I would have joined her.
Even as a read Seuss, I wonder how I got so lucky.

I wait for him as checks the house, turning off lights and securing locks.
I am showered and perfumed.

I wear something comfortable but far from warm.
And I feel loved.

He brings me ice water and a beer and we talk as he sits on the edge
of the bed.

He knows
and I know
that if he should undress and crawl in
the things that need to be discussed
would never even be
remembered.

He leaves to shower,
and I wait.

I wonder
how did I get so lucky?

PAUL PETILLO

We have never made love the same way twice.

We've done it
in familiar places
at familiar times,
but never the same way.

Our inventiveness
is largely the result of the foreplay we have engaged,
throughout the day.

The little things we have said
to each other,
or the way we said them,
all create this electrified atmosphere
we slip into
when we are together.
With
every
whispery touch
or
hitched breath, she shows me,
that,
like me, we have waited all day for this.

She is many women and they all adore me.

We never schedule this time,
instead,
we promise it, stolen from the chaotic clock that
governs our lives.

I t's like
          'if I don't get it, I will die.'

All
day
long
he teases me with his words and phrasing,
knowing
the frustrated state of passion he is giving me.

And when I finally get him alone,
I
can
hardly
contain
myself.

I become what he needs,
and what we share stops time. There is
passion and love,
lust and tenderness,
fever and calm.

We become
mythological. He becomes
fantasies I could never imagine.
And it will be like nothing that has happened… ever
before.

I can't talk afterward.
I can't think
or move.
She smiles and snuggles and kisses me
In case she falls asleep.

She will.
Her world is right,
and that makes me very happy.

Her world
is my world
is our world.

I've married all
that heaven
will allow.

I love us.

He and I are a we.

And we are good.
We are happy and sad as a we.
We are rich and poor as a we.
We are hot and sweaty as a we.

We love us
and the rest of the world is on its own.

I kiss him
In case I fall asleep,
and wrap myself in his warmth.

He lays there with
This silly grin on his face
And not a thought in his head.
His mind is at ease.
His body is relaxed.
His spirit is at peace.
And that makes me happy.

I can look forward to tomorrow as long as he is in it.

PAUL PETILLO

I love you.

I love you, too.

ON THE PORCH; UNDERNEATH.

I

"Oh, the news today was bad.
How bad could it be, you ask?
It was sad,
in a way that makes that makes me happy you're
not here.

I swore I'd never get to the point where
where,
where I'd be talking to you as if you were still sitting
next to me. I swore that once.

And yet, here this old fool is,
Doing it nonetheless.
-I do miss you.

You'd be proud of me though.
I still get up in the morning,
Still make my breakfast,
Still do the watering-
Although that's become quite the challenge of late.

You remember how my eyes was failing when you
was failing
And we was both hoping we.

I still talk about us as a we. Is that okay?

Would people say I was nuts, or crazy, or an old loon?
And you'd say, in a voice that I miss so much,
"Why, Jide, do you even care what they think?"

I'd tell you just like I be telling you right now,
I just don't want to think I was watering the bushes
and instead be giving the neighbor's car a rinse off.

You'd laugh.

I can see you standing at the bedroom window,
That was when you could stand at the window.
That was when I could see things clear.
That was when.

You'd laugh.
You wouldn't say nothing.
You'd just laugh.

God, I miss that laugh.

Anyway, things have gotten bad, Adora."

II

"I'm having a hell of a time.
I am. Helluva time. Hell might be better than this
damp, dirt floor.

If hell is hot, like the brimstone serenade I have
been force-fed,
It would be a welcome embrace.
But I don't believe.

"seek not the things that are too high for thee," the
good book says.

Their good book.

But seeking something higher than what I have become
to be
to be something, someone, someplace different.

They think I don't know, don't reason, although.

All men are not drawn to God.
I have received the direction,
An end that surpasses the argument of reason.

"The eye hath not seen, O God, besides Thee, what

things Thou hast prepared for them that wait for Thee," the good book says.

Their good book.
O God.

I am not a man of prayer.
I was a man of prayer.
I sought the divinity.
I practiced.

Am I the admixture of errors that prevents the revelation? The philosophy suggests I am imperfect.
Imperfect.
Yes, God, look at me. Imperfect.

It wasn't always like this.
There was a time,
when I would rise before each dawn, each dawn rising before the household.
I would count the minutes of slipping solitude, the bustle of the day unfolding.
The regularity.

The stuff I was supposed to be thankful for, or, driven to prayer, driven by the, what? Beauty?

It's not so beautiful now.

There was that time,
When thoughts of other men, writing to prompt me,
In the words of,
"For many things are shown to thee above

the understanding of man," the good book said.

Their good book.

I stood,
pulpit between me and them and supposedly,
allegedly,
behind me was the inconvenience of faith,

The easiness to twist a thought,
to make you wonder who and when.

Aquinas argued.
It didn't help me.
But it might help you.

The earth is round. Science. Math says so. The physi-
cist is in agreement.
Science is also philosophy.
Therefore, theology is sacred doctrine.
Because, and I look at the faces.
They look back

They keep looking back.

My words hang.

They don't know what happened to me.
That would be a revelation.

I don't shout it. I don't say it.

"For many things are shown to thee above the
understanding of man," the good book said.

Their good book.

If hell is not hot. Is hell damp?"

III

"I'm sorry, Adora.
You were the one that kept my breath,
The air you stole from me, the gasp of delight
at the sight of you,
walking into a room,
or

Working those beans everybody asked you to bring.
and you'd always say,
'it's Jide, on the smoker'

And they'd look at me.
And I'd look away because you never taught me how
to not be embarrassed
by the limelight,
by the things most folk like to be recognized for
having done.

You never taught me.

I never learned, was more like it.
One day, I'm going to go looking through your
things.
For that box;
the one with my breath, you stole.

But not now, or later, or tomorrow. It is still too, too soon. Way too soon.

So many sentences begin, I remember that time.

And that's how I think about each day.
Preacher tells me,
he came by to check,
Yesterday, the day before. Not really sure.

He was looking a fit as a fiddle if'n someone who weighs five hundred pounds
could look fit as a fiddle.

More like a stand-up bass. Did that make you laugh, Adora?

He brought up your beans.
I cried. Not in front of him.
In front of him, I just agreed how damn good they was.

I think he was hungry, Adora.
I think he was expecting I would have done what you'd have done and offered him something.

You never taught me that I had to carry on.

You never said I'd have to be strong. I'm not.

Not anymore.

I think he was hungry, Adora. The girl next door brings me groceries;
And puts them away,

and checks on me.
Just like you asked her to do.

Not sure whether she feels sorry for me,
or loved you so much,
or she knows I won't last long.

Not without you.

You never taught me."

IV

"What is hell, and am I supposed to do with this?

"Wisdom gave him the knowledge of holy things,"
the good book said.
Their good book.

The descent is perilous and yet,
It is by far the easiest journey I have ever taken.

No one who told me one foot in front of the other
was the only thing I had to do.
Not sidestep,
Not hop or skip or jump,
Not.

Do what I did.
And I'm still unsure what I did. Or how.

I'm supposed to reflect.
When life skewers you, like it skewered me, intro-
spection is the next station. Via Crucis.
My Ways of Sorrow.

Who knew how fragile?
Holding it the way a child holds a snow globe.
With every adult in the room wondering,

Will he drop it?
Can the little hands of the boy understand the
weight?
The memories the object holds,
More than the scene inside, some snow on a village
you'd never been,
representing,
a simpler time?
a better time?
the time before the skewering?

I know now. Shake it and watch the magical chaos
entreat the image.

I once suggested that God was first. Ha!
That credit for all the creatures belonged to him,
first.

So, why did he take my creatures?
It wasn't very practical.

I'm no Job but I can see a well-orchestrated effort. It
wasn't very practical.
Or lyrical.

Here's where the confusion ensues.
There is sacred doctrine - and that's supposed to be
practical.
Sacred doctrine is God - and that's because we're
handiwork.
God knows himself - and we're supposed to prefect
knowledge.
He wants us scriptured - and we are profanely eru-

dite.
Perfect knowledge of God - and we'll have eternal bliss.

This is not bliss. This is hopelessness and a damp floor."

V

"Do you remember that four leaf clover I found?
You said, "Jide!"
As if it where the sun and the moon.
As if it were a bouquet of flowers
As if it were as precious as the ring.

I found the ring, Adora. It was pressed into the same
book,
The one I gave you,
because you said that book was your absolute

Your very best,
Your word crush,
author and
you just had to have it.

And I sought the man who wrote it,
chased him down in his white suburb, oh, how you
chastised me when you heard that.

But you had to have it. I was the one
who came up with the cockamamy idea to get it
signed.

I didn't get hurt. No police. So, I guess it turned out

okay.

The ring,
Aluminum and flattened by the pages.
It was the last book that author ever wrote.
I didn't size it.
I guessed it would fit.
And it did.
And you cried.
And you saved it.

I don't know what made me pick it up.
I can't do no more reading.
And you know how I loved doing it.
The fuzzy stuff on my eyes,
Well,
It helps me too. It helps not see the blank space you
left me.

I pretend you're in the next room, shuffling some-
thing or simply laughing at the TV,
but, I don't go in there to prove you're not.
The TV's not on of course.
I could turn it on, I suppose.
For sound.

But I'd miss whatever it is you might say. Feel free to
say something.
Anything.

You put it between wax paper.
You thought I had a special talent for finding them.

I'd explain my technique,

and you'd listen,
every time,
and pretend I'd never explained before.

But you're not going to answer.
Did I ever tell you how much I enjoyed the way you
said my name?

So, French.
Accent on the last syllable. Like I did with your
name.
Accent on the soft a. AdorA. Ah, like satisfied.

I didn't know what to do with the book,
or why I picked it up.
I do recall holding it for a long time.

I use the same fork, knife, spoon, plate, bowl, and
pan repeatedly.
I wash 'em by hand.
I leave them on the rack to dry.

I can't bring myself to open the cabinets.

Like the book.

I shouldn't have opened it."

VI

"It happened so fast.

This, haunts me:

"yet the slenderest knowledge that may be obtained of the highest things is more desirable than the most certain knowledge obtained of lesser things."
Aristotle. de Animalibus xi.

Don't ask.
It haunts me nonetheless.

In the absence of answers, and in the absence of listeners,
you need them to ask questions
even if they are of a lesser knowledge, they try to grapple.
Is that a word that suits the struggle on their faces? I see it. They grapple.

One minute, and then another, and here I am. That fast.

Not to denounce the possibility that it was revelation.

God might have,
no, he probably did have,
his celestial sacredness somewhere in the mix.

It wouldn't surprise me.

Nothing does anymore.
I'm one of those lesser things who succumbs to the
pull of natural reason.

"This is your wisdom and understanding in the
sight of nations," the good book said.
Their good book.

But I don't feel.
I don't feel anything. It's kind of weird, I suppose.

So, the homily went south when I discussed wisdom.
There's an argument, and that is what I called it,
because conflict was the wrong word,
although I'm definitely conflicted, more so now. It
was an argument.

Isn't all great philosophy?
For future reference, I probably should not have
brought up the subject.
But I did. I likened my wisdom to that of the archi-
tect.
I likened my parishioners to the laborers.

The lesser things shuffled in their seats.

And I missed that obvious reaction.

I tend to get swept into my oratory and assume, everyone else is as well. Swept.

A single voice. It followed this, "Wisdom is prudence to a man," from the good book.
Their good book.

You're not God.

It happened pretty fast after that."

VII

"I wished I had written every word you ever said,
wrote it down,
saved it,
saved it so I could read it again.

But that didn't happen, Adora, and now,
well,
now, it's just a voice rattling around in an old man's
head.

Do you remember that time we went to the beach?
You sang. I don't remember the song.
My eyes, my ears, they filled with tears.
And all I see is you, that flowered dress.

It's bad, you know.
Life without you.

So many people miss you.
The ladies from the church came 'round the other
day.

I almost didn't answer the door. Your door. The one
you opened for me,
everyday. Smiling. Everyday. Home from work.

When I was working.

I didn't want to.
I didn't want to participate.
I didn't want to go out and compete with all those
other
but I did it for you,
and I didn't want to be friendly
but I did it for you.
I didn't want to.
But there was something in your eyes that suggested I'd be a better man for it.
Because of it.

Despite me being who me was. Under my breath, I
may have said, "Damn you, woman."
You were right.
I was wrong.
I am sorry. Is it too late to say I'm sorry.

The church ladies went away, eventually.
I couldn't do it.
I couldn't let them walk away, so I rushed to open
the door before they got in their car.

Adora, they miss you too.

I didn't want to.
I didn't want to share you.
And now, I wish I hadn't been so selfish,
Sometimes brutish in my jealousy. You belonged to
everyone.

You were the gift."

VIII

"I did not take kindly to judgment.

Not from them,
not like that.

Judgment appertains to wisdom. I know this. I ascribe to this.

How dare they, he, she, whoever.

"The spiritual man judgeth all things," the good book said.
Their good book.
The same one I use, once used.
No more.

One can judge by inclination.

They were so inclined, to be considered virtuous, to be able to incline judgment.
They were not knowledgeable. No.

I waved my arm to them. Sweeping. Priestly. Grandly sweeping.

I was used to being right.
"Put arguments aside where faith is sought," the

good book said.
Their good book.

But they don't read what they don't agree with.
Revelation?
Argument?

I did what I had to do.
The homily would have included,
"embrace that faithful word which is according to
doctrine,
that he may be able to exhort in sound doctrine
and to convince the gainsayers," the good book said.
Their good book.
And I am that word.

I'm still convinced.
Even as I sit on this cold, dark, damp dirt floor,
crouched like an animal.

Listening to the man above.***"***

IX

"I hear you down there." I finally said it, Adora.
I didn't want to say it.
I sit on this porch,
In the morning I watch the kids, packed off to
school.
In the middle of the day, I see the heat shimmer
from the blacktop.
In the dinner hour, I take my plate, the same plate
and fork and knife.
In the dark, I count fireflies. Just like you did.

I could hear the talking,
The sad refrain of something distant.
At first, I thought it was distant.
But then, I thought it was inside me.
Mumbling.
In my voice.
Saying.

Adora, I was disturbed by what I heard in those mo-
ments.
Scripture.
What, my beloved, is scripture doing in my head?

I really appreciate what you didn't say. As much as I
miss all that you did.
Say.

You didn't tell me to do anything for you with your
last moments.
I wish you did.
But I'm glad you didn't.

I know, when a guy at the office said his wife wanted
him to move on, live.
I thought her cruel.
There she must've been.
Dying.
Apparently, she died for a long time.
Dying.
Days.
And then she makes a last request.

Prisoners make last requests before they are exe-
cuted.
It's not the same.
It can't be the same.
It shouldn't be the same.

It wasn't the same with you.

Should I be?
Sad? That you didn't.
Happy? That you didn't.

But you were still cruel.

You made me a better man, and I wanted no part of
that.
You taught me to listen, and now I wish,
I had written every word you said, down, somewhere, etched.

They were your last requests. Not at your last
breath. Not then.
Every breath you took.

I realized the scripture wasn't in my head.
You tried.
You really tried.
But none of it stuck. All of it stuck.
I stomp my foot.

"Hey, you. You hungry?"

X

"In the darkness,
there is a solitude and a fear, acting against my faith.

Am I a heretic?
I feel as one. Here in the darkness.
Am I Hus?

Uncharacteristically, they shouted back. I stood stunned.
"Christ bore a far heavier"
I pause. A far heavier.
"Crown of Thorns."

I picture Hus. His paper crown. His paper devils.

It's dark, and moist, and this is how hell should be.
Uncomfortable.
So they cast me out.
They casted out Hus as well.
So I was half-naked.
They stripped Hus and marched him off to execution.
So I asked to confess.
They would not let Hus do so.
So they called me a heretic.

"Heretics are not be given privilege."

I cannot argue but with an argument.
Deny one principle.
Argue another.

"They that explain me shall have life everlasting,"
the good book said.
Their good book.

I tell them. Repeatedly.
Above the din.
"God provides for everything."

I leave out the part about capacity. They lack it.

I just shake my head. I bow my head. I am a revelation.

In the dark, the sky above me thuds.
I cower.
Poets, I think at the very moment, represent with metaphor.
A representation.
The Holy Writ believes they rise to truth.

Another thud.

And a voice, I know. I've heard it.
I hoped it would whisper me.
Just once.

Affirm.
"Give not that which is holy to dogs," the good book said.

PAUL PETILLO

Their good book.

Timidly, "I am hungry."

XI

"You have raised me to be kind, Adora.
And I should despise you for that. I have tried might-
ily.
Strenuously.

And failed to unlearn what I learned.

I just can't see myself as kind, Adora.
Without feeling the hypocrite.
I am moral.
I know right from wrong and know wrong ain't
right.
The only law be served,
is the law to not harm the weak,
as you said, so sweetly,
no, Jide, you said,
an eye for an eye is not right,
not wrong, but not right.

Is there any one word, she asked,
she asked. Choose one,
and be bound by reciprocity,
its truth, Jide, and principle of high regard.

I just can't see myself as kind, Adora.

But I ask the man under the porch if he's hungry.

Nonetheless."

XII

"Suppose,"
I detest that word.
From the pew, he yells,
"nobler bodies are not worthy to explain."

As I have sought to do.
Badly, evidently.

He's quoting Dionysius. Three things.
Not from Dionysius. From Thomas Aquinas.
But he called me nobler.
A man of their cloth, borne of their needs.
Three things.
The less noble a man the better that man's mind is
preserved from error.
I make no error.
He is what he is and no man can explain that. God is
above whatsoever.
Still, I make no error.
Those so-called divine truths, the ones I have de-
voted myself to, are better hidden,
from the unworthy.
From you, I want to yell back.
Still, I made no error.

The unworthy suffer,
Literal,
Allegorical
Tropological
Anagogical
All shortcomings.

You have to believe,
and I do not, that the Holy Writ is God's handiwork.

I'm supposed to, and they yell asking me to suppose.
Things are words are literal.
Do things for Christ and you have allegory.

I look at him, his face is impoverished. How does
one explain analogy?
I look at his family, his friends, his fellow parishioners. They think me a heretic.

The thud on ceiling is not God.

And I cannot answer, the man calls me to the table,
and I can't go.
I won't go.

I'm not here.
"The fool said in his heart, There is no God," the
good book said.
Their good book.

I am hungry, I feel that pain.
But I cannot go to him.
I feel his pain, and that of my accuser.

But I cannot go to them with salve.
I do not belong to their salvation.

I yell, but he doesn't hear me. I'm not here."

XIII

"You are not an animal, Jide."

I feel as though I am the essence of one. Though.
Sufficient.
Perhaps more.
Clever,
Stupid,
Gullible.

I listened to that preacher of yours. The one you
liked, Adora.
Brimstone and holy battlefields ablaze with the
good fight.

I ask you why we are fighting.
You don't answer. I'm your heretic. And I think
it embarrassed you.

I feel child-like in the presence of your faith. You
won't, can't refuse to.
I act churlish at times. I need a demonstration.

"It cannot be done, Jide," you say as you work your
magic with scrambled eggs.
"Butter," you tell me,

avoiding the answer I will not accept.
Instead, folding it into, and over, wrist motion,
smiling, you say, in the gentlest of voices,
"Eggs when eggs hold infinite possibilities.
Eggs broken, hold finite possibilities." Folding,
And over, wrist motion.

Smiling still, you say, to the child who is arguing
what he cannot see,
"All things, therefore, that have been delivered to us
by Law,"
she adds, still smiling,
"and Prophets and Apostles and Evangelists we re-
ceive,
and know,
and honor,
seeking for nothing beyond these."
Still, folding it in and over,
wrist motion.

"For God, being good, is the cause of all good,"
She turns to me and smiles,
"subject neither to envy nor to any passion."

It is her smile.
Adora looks nothing like the whale-sized reverend.
Nothing like the women who   came by the
other day.

I know there is no one below the porch.
No heretical priest.

I took dinner to the front porch,

again.
Alone,   again.

I'll try to do better, Adora."

ABOUT THE AUTHOR

Paul Petillo has a long and diverse resume that doesn't always correctly portray his wide-ranging interests. In 1999, he opened a financial education center online and focused on the difficulty the average person faced when looking for information on personal finances, investing, insurance, and buying a home. The information was there, but it was often associated with a company looking to sell you their product. BlueCollarDollar.com offered an in-depth look into these products and offered his millions of readers a wealth of information about suitability. He handcrafted the site, writing all of the code and publishing over 2,800 articles.

In 2002, McGraw-Hill approached him and asked if he would consider writing a book that took his website to the printed word. In 2004, Building Wealth in a Paycheck-to-Paycheck world was published during a contentious election season and did reasonably well. Three additional books were written for McGraw-Hill over the next three years.

Over the next decade, he appeared on television, radio, hosted his radio show, and contributed to numerous financial websites. Unfortunately, the internet was changing (going mobile, offering user security, etc.). As the sole proprietor of the BCD, those changes would be incredibly time-consuming; the site was not equipped to make those changes and closed down in 2014.

He switched genres and began a fictional trilogy about a reclusive philanthropist with a very troubled past. The Scourge of Princes saw his protagonist come of age in the first novel of the same title, but researched by a local newspaper reporter forty years later in Invisible Cities, and come to terms with his dark past in Saint Aretino.

In 2020, he published a collection of novellas in a book titled Blue Pond. These diverse tales include a story of germline chimerism and adoption titled I Can Be You. The search for missing diamonds stolen decades ago is the focus of the book's title story, Blue Pond, written for those who enjoy a mystery. And lastly, the unexpected conclusion to the trilogy he had previously written where the title character is a disgruntled employee called The Obitist.

Whisper Me is his first work of poetry.

He is married to Bonnilyn, his wife of 36 years, and lives in Portland. All of his works can be found at paulpetillo.com